María Tolete

A Venezuelan folktale illustrated by Irene Savino

HOUGHTON MIFFLIN COMPANY

BOSTON

Atlanta   Dallas   Geneva, Illinois

Palo Alto   Princeton   Toronto

María Tolete comes from the oral tradition of Venezuela. It contains many elements of well-known fairy tales, especially the tale of Cinderella.

Rafael Olivares Figueroa (1893–1973) retold this story in his book *Folklore Venezolano* (Venezuelan Folklore).

This version of *María Tolete* is by Verónica Uribe, an editor for the Venezuelan publishing house Ediciones Ekaré – Banco del Libro.

Irene Savino is an illustrator and designer who lives in Venezuela. She teaches at the Institute of Design in Caracas.

This version of "María Tolete" originally appeared in *CUENTOS LEYENDAS DE AMOR PARA NIÑOS*, Copyright © 1984 by Ediciones Ekaré-Banco del Libro, Venezuela. Text translated and reprinted by special arrangement with Ediciones Ekaré. Translation Copyright © 1993 by Houghton Mifflin Company. Illustrations by Irene Savino Copyright © 1993 by Houghton Mifflin Company

Houghton Mifflin Edition, 1993.

Printed in the U.S.A.

ISBN 0-395-61795-2

456789-B-96 95 94 93

María Tolete

One day, a poor and hungry girl walked out of the rain
forest that surrounded a hacienda in Venezuela. She
silently appeared at the back door of the largest house on
the plantation.

The girl was so frail, she looked like a little twig ready
to snap. The servants felt sorry for her. They gave her
food and drink that day, and the next day, and the next...

Before long it was as if she had always been there,
living quietly in forgotten corners of the hacienda. No one
but the servants knew of the pitiful little girl—not even the
landlady, who owned the hacienda.

One afternoon, some of the young men and young women of the hacienda noticed the poor girl for the first time. They asked her what her name was. She answered in her soft voice: "María."

Laughing, the young men formed a circle around her and started taunting: "María Tolete, María the Twig! María Tolete, María the Twig!"

From then on, María tried even harder to keep herself hidden away.

But a night came when the full moon shone in the sky, and the landlady's handsome son was getting dressed to go to a dance. At the door to his room appeared María the Twig.

"Please," she said, "take me with you to the dance."

The young man was dumbstruck.

"You? Dance with me?" he hollered. "That's enough of that! Go iron my shirt. And hurry! I need it for the dance!"

After the young man had left for the dance, María the
Twig hurried to a secret waterfall that was hidden in the
nearby rain forest. She bathed and perfumed herself
with the gentle herbs that grew there. Then she returned
to the house, borrowed a beautiful dress from the closet
of the landlady's daughter, and put up her long, black hair.

At the dance, everyone was dazzled by the beauty of a mysterious young woman in the beautiful dress. The men pushed and shoved each other for the chance to dance with her. The handsome son from the hacienda couldn't keep his eyes off her.

"I have never seen you before," he said to her at last. "Where are you from?"

"I come from far away, very far away," she answered. "I am from the city of Iron." But the young man was so enchanted by her that he paid no attention to her strange answer.

When the young man went back home he could not stop talking about the mysterious girl he had seen at the dance. He spent the next few days searching for her throughout the neighboring towns, but he could not find her. He almost wept from frustration.

Ten nights later, when the moon was hidden from view, the young man was invited to another dance. Just as before, María the Twig appeared in his room and said to him in her sweet voice, "Please, take me with you."

Again, the young man began to yell. "You? Dance with me? That's enough of that! Go fetch my coat. And hurry! I need it for the dance!"

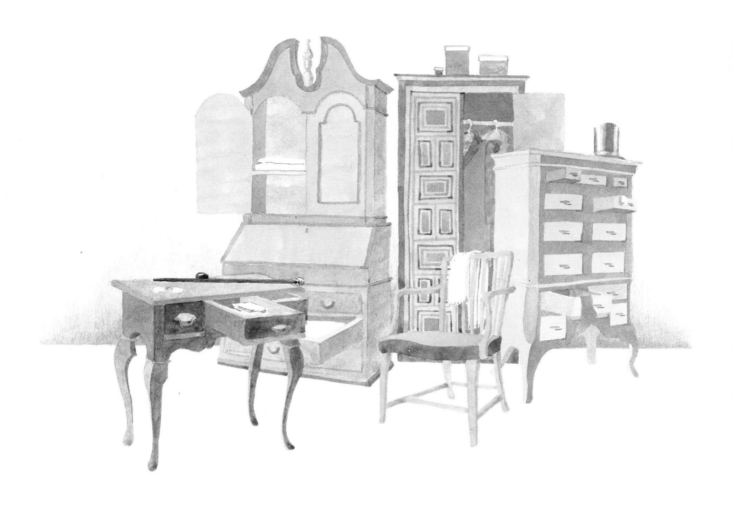

After the young man had left, María the Twig hurried to the waterfall, bathed herself, put on another dress that belonged to the landlady's daughter, and put up her long, black hair.

Once again, at the dance everyone was dazzled by the beauty of this mysterious young woman. The hacienda owner's son approached her and, sighing, said, "Tell me, where are you from?"

"I come from far away, very far away," she answered. "I am from the city of Fetch." But as before, the lovestruck young man paid no attention to her strange answer.

Ten nights later, as the half moon rose in the sky, the young man was invited to another dance. For the third time, María the Twig appeared in his room and said to him in her sweet voice, "Please, take me with you."

And for the third time the young man yelled, "You? Dance with me? That's enough of that! Go shine my shoes. And hurry! I need them for the dance!"

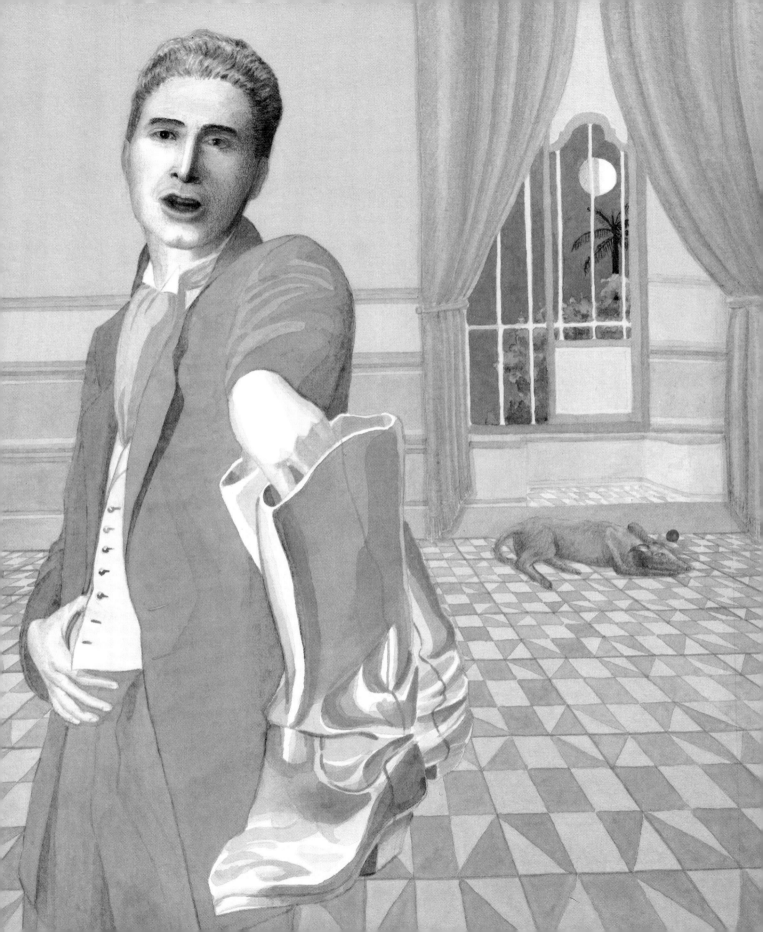

    Once again, after the young man had left, María the Twig dressed herself radiantly and appeared at the dance. Once again, everyone was dazzled by her beauty. The young man danced with her, while whispering loving words, and gave her a ring as a gift. For the third time he asked, "Please, tell me, where are you from?"

    "I come from far away, very far away," she answered. "I am from the city of Shine."

    But the young man was so dizzy with love for her that as before he paid no attention to her strange words.

Upon returning home, the young man woke up everyone in the household to tell them about the mysterious girl. The next day he searched the hacienda and the nearby towns again, but he could not find her.

The young man felt so sad that he became ill. No prayers could help him regain his strength. He was so utterly sad that he was close to dying.

María the Twig asked the landlady's permission to make cornmeal porridge for the sick young man.

The landlady was insulted. "How dare you think my son will like the porridge you make, little girl! He only likes the porridge his mother makes!"

But María the Twig pleaded so long that the landlady finally gave in.

So María the Twig prepared the cornmeal porridge, and when no one was looking, she slipped the ring that the young man had given her into the bowl.

As he drank the porridge, the young man sighed, "This cornmeal is delicious, mother!" Then, when he discovered the ring, he was filled with amazement. "Mother," he said, "who made this porridge?"

"María the Twig made it. Why do you ask? Is there something wrong with it?"

Before the young man could answer, there stood María the Twig in his room, wearing a beautiful dress, her long, black hair shining, her face glowing.

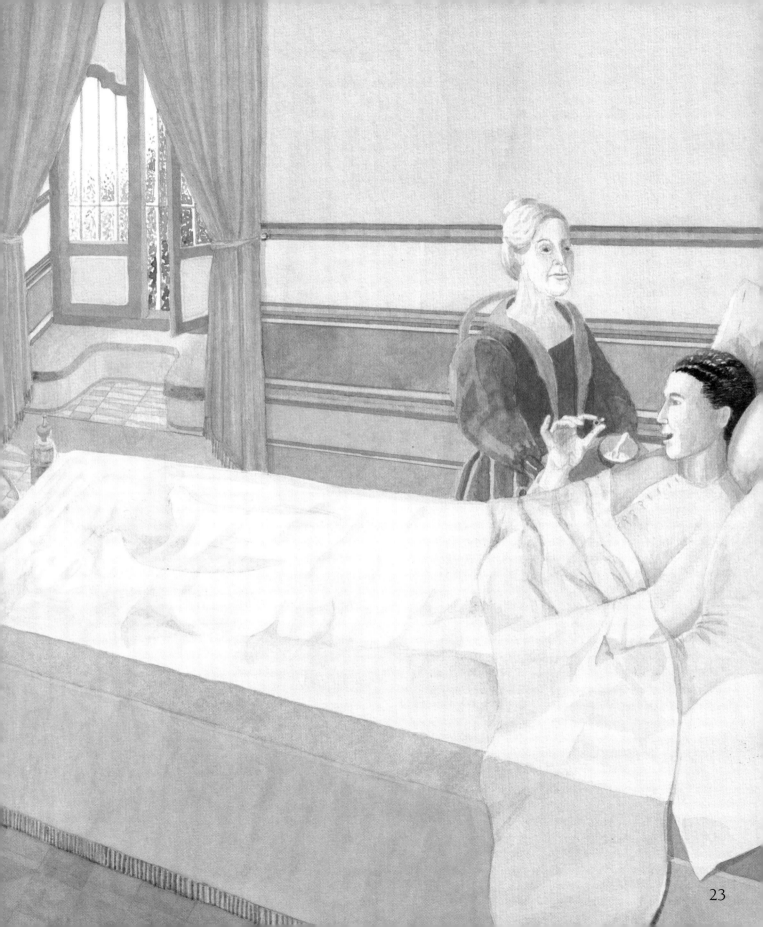

Instantly, the young man was cured. Despite his mother's objections, he married María. Soon the young man's mother came to love María the Twig, too, and the couple lived happily ever after on a beautiful hacienda of their own in Venezuela.